The Chameleon's True Colors

Juliya Pankratova

FAMILIUS

Published by Familius LLC, www.familius.com

PO Box 1249, Reedley, CA 93654

Familius books are available at special discounts for bulk purchases,
whether for sales promotions or for family or corporate use.
For more information, email orders@familius.com.
Reproduction of this book in any manner, in whole or in part,
without written permission of the publisher is prohibited.

Library of Congress Control Number: 2020950044
Print ISBN 9781641704489
Ebook ISBN 9781641704991
KF: 9781641705196
FE: 9781641705394
Printed in China

Edited by Michele Robbins
Cover and design by Carlos Guerrero

10 9 8 7 6 5 4 3 2 1

First Edition

Deep in the jungle, there lived . . .

. . . a little chameleon.

He had scaly skin, a swirly tail, googly eyes,

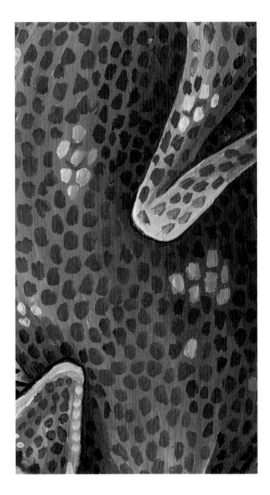

and a loooooooooong tongue.

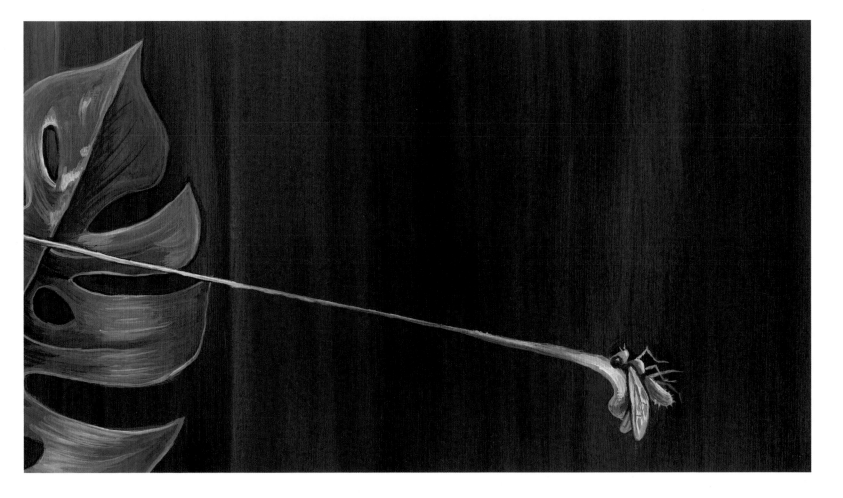

But the chameleon was missing something very important.

He did not have a color!
So, one day, he set off to find it.

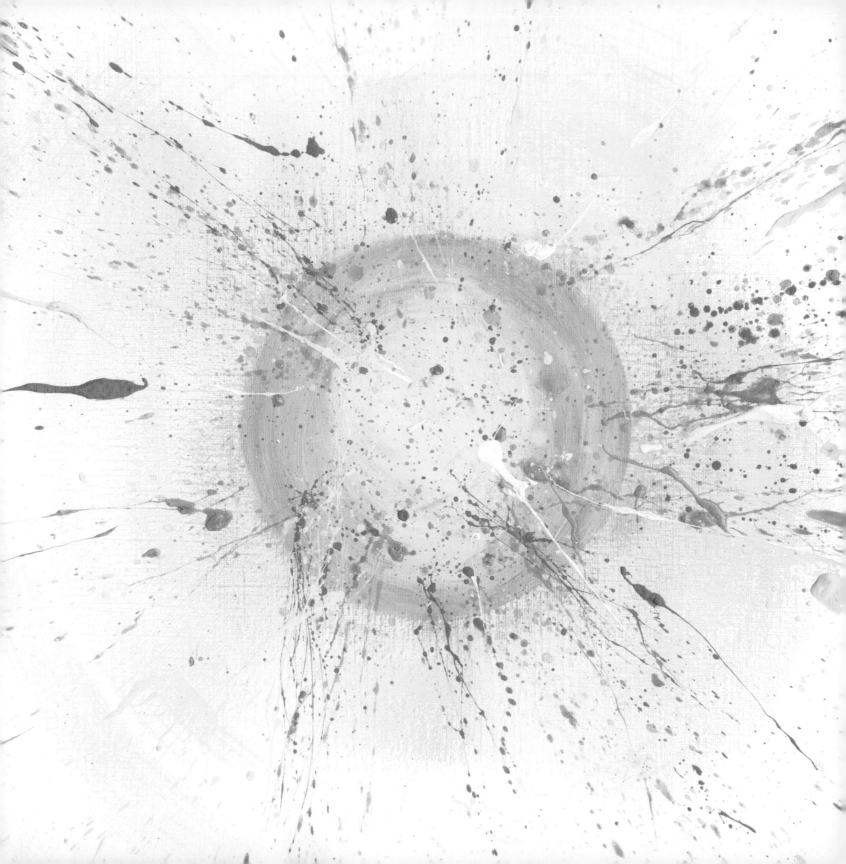

First, the chameleon looked up to the bright sky.
"Hello, sun!" he called. "I like your color. What is it?"

"Hello, little chameleon. My color is yellow!
It lights up the world."

"Wow! I want to light up the world too!"

Next, the chameleon looked down to the jungle floor.

"Hello, orchid!" he said.
"I like your color. What is it?"

"Hello, little chameleon.
My color is pink. It makes the bees dance around me."

"Awww . . . I want the bees to dance around me too!"

Suddenly, something bright
landed next to the chameleon.

"Hello, ladybird!" he said. "I like your color. What is it?"

"Hello, little chameleon. My color is spotted red.
It warns the birds not to eat me."

"Eeek! I want to warn
the birds not to eat me too!"

Then, the chameleon heard a
rustling in the tall grass behind him.

"Oh! Hello there, tiger!" he said. "I like your color. What is it?"

"Hello, little chameleon. My color is striped orange. It helps me to hide in the grass."

"Fun! I want to hide in the grass too!"

Just then, something soft brushed past the chameleon.

"Hello, peacock!" he said. "I *really* like your color. What is it?"

"Hello, little chameleon. I have two colors: green and blue. I use them to impress my friends."

"Ooh-la-la! I want to impress my friends too!"

"WOW! Look at me, everyone!" cried the little chameleon.

But when he turned to his friends, he saw . . .

The chameleon's new colors weren't his after all.
He couldn't keep them now, could he?

So, he returned
the sun's yellow,

the orchid's pink,

the tiger's
striped orange,

and the peacock's
blue and green.

the ladybird's
spotted red,

"Thank you for returning our colors, little chameleon," his friends said. "We will share them with you whenever you want."

And that is how the little chameleon deep in the jungle can change his color whenever he likes.